ON THE
RUN

RL 3.0 - 4.5

ON THE RUN

by

T. ERNESTO BETHANCOURT

Developed by Cebulash Associates
Design by Square Moon Productions
Cover Photo by Richard Hutchings

1-55855-697-4

1

The trouble with me, I think, is that I don't listen when people tell me things. Everyone said I should fly to California. I took a train. It cost more to take the train, but I thought maybe I could see more of the country. Did I ever! You know what there is between the small town in Missouri, where I'm from, and Los Angeles? Right—more land than I wanted to see.

On top of that, food on a train costs an arm and a leg. I was going to get to L.A.

with maybe $20 in my jeans. Sure, I had work waiting for me. I even had an uncle who would put me up until I got my own place. Maybe he could lay a few dollars on me until I got paid. I only hoped that he would be there to meet me, like he said he would. He comes and goes pretty often because of his job. He is an FBI agent.

I know that sounds strange. You see all those shows on TV and you never think that an FBI guy might have a family. Uncle Larry is my dad's younger brother. He went into the FBI after he got back from Vietnam. My dad was there too, but he got back before Uncle Larry. Dad came home to Missouri and his old job. Larry stayed in California.

Dad got sick from something they used to kill plants in Vietnam. He died when I was 12. After that, my mother got an office job, and with money from Uncle Sam and Uncle Larry, I got to finish my schooling. I learned to do body and paint work on cars. In California there is plenty of work for a body and paint man. So there I was at 21, headed for a new job in a new city.

The train was a half hour out of L.A. I was looking out the window at some run-down old buildings when I heard someone crying softly. I looked across the aisle, and there was this girl. I would say she was about 20. Nice-looking girl, I thought, if she didn't have a red nose and eyes. I should have kept my mouth shut, I know.

"Are you all right?" I asked. She turned her face away. "Don't be that way," I said. "You look like a nice girl in trouble. I wondered if I could help."

"No one can help," she said. "Or do you have something to eat? Or some clean clothes for me?"

"Come on, don't feel bad," I said. "We get into L.A. in a half hour. I'm sure there is a coffee shop or something at Union Station."

"That won't do me any good," she said. "I went to sleep last night, and when I got up, my bag was gone. It had all my clothes and money in it!" She started to cry again.

"Don't you know anyone in L.A.?" I asked.

"I'm not going to Los Angeles," she said. "I have to get a bus there to take me to where I'm really going. It is a place about 50 miles away."

"Can't you phone and have someone pick you up?"

"I'm going to my dad's," she said. "He is sick and doesn't drive. I had a bus ticket, but it was in my bag, too."

I did what most of people would think was dumb. I mean, how many times have you heard people say, "Never give money to someone you don't know"? But like I said, I'm not a good listener. I know you must think I'm some kind of soft touch. I reached into my pocket and counted up what I had: almost $20. I knew Uncle Larry was going to pick me up. "How much would the bus ticket be?" I asked.

"It costs $18," she said, red eyed.

"OK," I said, as I took out my notebook and my pen. "My name is Jim Singer. This is where I'll be staying for a while." I wrote down Uncle Larry's name and number and address in Pasadena. I handed her the money and the piece of paper from my book. "When you get to your dad's, you can send me the money."

"No, I can't take your money," she said.

"Don't be dumb," I said. "I have someone meeting me. I'll be all right. Maybe we can see each other once I get a payday and some wheels."

"But you don't even know me."

"Easy enough," I said, as I put out my hand. "You know my name. What is yours?"

"Susan . . . Susan Conway," she said. She smiled and the car seemed brighter. She took my hand. I had been right. She was great looking when she wasn't crying. She had deep blue eyes, even teeth, and clear skin. "I live in Simi Valley," she said. "That is . . . ."

"About 50 miles from L.A.," I finished. "You told me."

She pulled the paper I gave her in half. Then she took my pen and wrote down where she lived. "I *will* send the money back to you, Jim," she said.

"How about if I come and pick it up?" I asked. "Maybe we could see a movie . . . have a bite to eat."

"I think I would like that," she said.

By the time we got to Union Station, we knew a little bit about each other. And what I knew about her, I liked. She had been going to school back east, when her dad got sick. The money for her school ran out with her dad out of work. Her mother had died when she was little, and her dad was alone. Now she was going home to get a job and take care of her father.

When we got off the train, we said we would stay in touch. She headed for where the buses stop, and I went into the big part of the building to look for Uncle Larry.

Maybe you have seen Union Station in old movies on TV. The place was put up before everybody took jets . . . when the whole world went by train. Today, the station does not get much play. Half the time it is almost empty. And because the place is so big, it gives you a strange feeling, like most of the world died or went away.

I saw Uncle Larry right away. I had not seen him in years, but it was easy. He looks like Dad did, and that makes him look like me: six feet, dark hair, gray eyes, and heavy build. Maybe he isn't quite as heavy as I am. I used to work out when I was in high school. I was on the track team, too. I ran the 440 pretty fast, if I do say so myself.

"Jimmy, boy!" he yelled. He took my bag with one hand and shook my free hand with his other. "I'm so glad to see you. You grew up." He smiled and gave me a little punch on the arm. "How is your mother?"

"Just great, Uncle Larry," I said. "She said to say hello."

"Look, what is this 'Uncle Larry' about?"

he said. "You make me feel old. I'm your father's *younger* brother. And we're friends, so call me Larry." He started walking, and I followed. "My car is outside," he said. "We should be home in 40 minutes."

"I thought Pasadena was near by," I said.

"It is. But it is four o'clock. You can't drive anyplace at this hour. Any other time it would take 20 minutes. But up until six or seven o'clock, forget it."

We left the big station and walked a few blocks to the place where Larry had left his car. It was a 944 Porsche, silver with red leather inside. I was really going to like California, I thought. Maybe I could use the Porsche to go see Sue Conway.

Larry paid up, and we got out onto a street filled with cars. As we inched along, he said, "Got a surprise for you, Jim." He reached into his coat pocket and handed me a small box.

I opened it and stared. It was a gold, old-time Elgin wrist watch. "I know this watch," I said. "It was Dad's. But how did you get it? I thought my mother was keeping it."

"She was. She wanted to get it fixed, but she didn't have the money. She sent it to

11

me, and I had it made like new. Go ahead. Put it on. It is all yours."

"Thanks so much, Uncle—I mean, Larry," I said. "Soon as I get a payday, I'll pay you back."

"Think nothing of it," he said. "It is my present to you. I was . . . " He broke off.

"Something wrong, Larry?" I asked.

"I'm not sure," he said. He turned off onto a side street. There were almost no cars. It was a run-down part of town with old buildings. Most of them were boarded up. He looked back behind us. "But I'm sure now," he said. "There is a car following us. No, don't look around. It is a black Mercedes. Jim, I know this part of town well. I'm going to get rid of my tail."

"Does this have to do with your FBI work?" I asked.

"In a way," he said. "But you can't come with me, Jim." He went into his coat pocket and took out some papers and some keys. "This is what the man in the Mercedes is after. He will never think I would give them to you. Too important. When I get to that alley up there, I want you to get out of the car. I'll shake him and meet you back at Union Station in two hours. If I'm not back by then, I want you to go to my apartment in Pasadena."

"I don't know where that is," I said.

"Don't worry. Just ask. No more time to talk. Here comes that alley. Keep those papers in a safe pocket. Now go!"

He slowed down, and I opened the car door. He almost pushed me out. I hit the ground at a run. Larry burned rubber pulling away. The Mercedes came flying down the street right after him. I ducked down the alley. That is when I did another dumb thing. I turned to look.

The man behind the wheel was big, with dark hair cut short like a soldier's. He had a face like a rat. Just for a second, he looked my way and our eyes met. I don't know why, but I felt afraid. I'm not afraid of people. I have had my wars, and most of the time I have won. But there was something about this rat-faced man that shook me up. Then he was gone.

I stood there at the mouth of the alley. I thought I knew how to get back to Union Station. I started walking back. I had not gone far when I saw the black Mercedes on the way back. Larry shook him off all right. But now, Rat Face was after me!

2

I lucked out. He had not seen me. I moved through an alley and onto a busy street. My luck held. It was a one-way street, headed away from where the station was. Let Rat Face try to tail me now, I thought. I stayed near the buildings as I walked, waiting in doorways now and then to look around. Not a hide or hair of Rat Face or his car, but I didn't calm down until I was inside Union Station.

It wasn't until I was walking through the

big hall that I really thought about it. What if Larry could not get back? He had my bag in his car, and I didn't have a dollar in my jeans. I was no better off than Sue Conway had been. No sense in borrowing trouble. Sure, Larry would come back for me.

By eight o'clock it was clear Larry wasn't going to come back. Had Rat Face caught up with him? Or maybe Rat Face was right here in the station, watching me from some secret place. Maybe Larry could not take a chance on walking up to me. But if I hid in some corner, how would he find me?

I was starting to feel hungry. I felt inside my pocket and found the change I didn't give to Sue Conway: 45¢. Not even enough for a cup of coffee in this place. Maybe it was enough to call Larry's place in Pasadena.

I went to a phone, put in my change, and dialed Larry's number. On the fourth ring, his voice came over the wire: "Hello. This is Larry. I can't come to the phone just now, but leave your name and number . . . ." the machine went on.

"It is me, Jim," I began, then quit. I put the phone back on the hook and heard my last coins drop into the box. Now what?

I turned back and found a coffee shop off to one side of the big hall. There were a number of tables inside. I found an empty one and sat down. I was looking down at my feet and thinking dark thoughts when I heard a voice say, "Don't go to sleep, man. The police will put you right out on the street. They don't want street people staying in here."

I looked up. At the next table was this man about 40. He was turned out in a light silk suit with a yellow shirt and a dark tie. Gold rings with bright stones flashed on his fingers.

"I'm not sleeping," I said. "I'm waiting for a train."

The man laughed. "Sure you are. Don't try to fool old Bunny. I have seen enough people with no place to go. I know what they look like. I know what they *smell* like. You have 'no home' written all over you."

As Bunny was talking, a girl about Sue Conway's age came up to him. She could have been pretty, but she didn't look too clean and had dark rings under her eyes. She gave Bunny a folded bill—I didn't see how big. He reached into his pocket and gave her something. She looked around and then walked off fast. In that second, I knew what and who Bunny was.

He put the money in his coat pocket and turned back to me. "Don't look so down," he said, and he smiled at me. "Maybe I can help you out."

"I don't need any help," I said.

"Suit yourself," Bunny said. "Nice wristwatch you got there."

"It was my father's," I said.

"Give you $50 for it," Bunny said.

"What are you talking about?" I said. "It is worth six times that . . . maybe more."

"Not to me, man," Bunny said. "And I'm the only one around here buying."

I thought about the mess I was in. I had to get to Larry's place in Pasadena. Maybe once I got things straight with him, I could come back and get the watch. What else could I do? I took off the watch and gave it to Bunny. He reached into his pocket, came out with a big roll of bills, and handed me $50.

"Can I come here and buy it back from you?" I asked as Bunny put the watch on his wrist.

"Any time, man," Bunny said with a smile. "I'm here every night. Just ask for

Bunny. Everybody knows old Bunny."

"I'll be back," I told him.

"They all say that," Bunny answered.

I took the money and went to where the buses stop, just outside the station. In a few minutes, I was on my way to Pasadena. Trouble was, I didn't know where I was or where I was going. I had no idea how to find Larry's place. Outside of that, everything was just great.

The bus let me off in downtown Pasadena. I still had most of the $50 left, so I went into a coffee shop and had a light dinner. I also called a ride. There was no way I could find Larry's place on foot. The ride would cost me, but at least I would get where I was going.

My ride came in a few minutes, and the driver knew right away where Larry's place was. It turned out to be a big apartment building, not far away.

The driver was just about to stop when I saw the black Mercedes a few yards away from the front door of the place. "Don't stop," I said. "Go right by. Let me off in the next block."

When I got out, I crossed the street and came up behind the black Mercedes. Sure enough, there was Rat Face behind the wheel, watching the building. I wasn't sure he would know me. He had seen me for only a second, near that alley in L.A. I could not take any chances, though.

Most apartment houses have more than one way in and out. Larry's place wasn't any different. It took me some time walking around the block and looking in the dark, but I found a back way inside. It was the door to the washers and dryers. I looked at the paper with Larry's apartment number on it: 5-D. I took the car up to the right floor, put the key in the lock of 5-D, and walked inside. I wasn't ready for what I saw. FBI agents must make more than I thought. The place was right out of a movie.

I went to the window. It was a glass door, really. The apartment faced the street and there was a kind of porch outside. Slowly, I pulled the curtains to one side and looked down. The black car was still there. But I had no way of knowing if Rat Face was still inside it. I was feeling like I had been pretty sharp when I gave him the slip.

I went into the kitchen, which was full of the latest machines that people buy but never use. I got a cold drink and looked at the answering machine. The red light was flashing. I hit the start control and listened.

The first thing I heard was me, calling from Union Station. Then: "Jim, this is Larry. If you made it to my place, just stay put. Take very good care of those papers I gave you. If the phone rings, let the machine answer. Pick it up only if it is me calling. Stay away from the doors and windows. If no one knows you are there, you are in no danger. I'll call as soon as I can." The machine cut off.

I went into the front room and sat down. Larry had a fine 25-inch TV. I was thinking of watching it until he called back. That was when the door bell rang.

I froze and then edged up to the door. I put my eye to the little glass thing set in the door and found myself looking at Rat Face in the hall!

I moved away from the door as quietly as I could.

Then I heard Rat Face trying the door lock. I went to the glass door and moved silently out onto the porch. I shut the glass door behind me. I was only buying time; I knew that. Once Rat Face got inside, he was sure to check the porch.

I looked down five floors to the ground. Then I saw there was another porch, right under the one where I sat. I moved slowly over the edge and hung by my hands, trying not to think about the 60 feet of thin air below. Just as I heard the glass door open above me, I let go and landed on the porch below.

3

I stood there, listening to myself breathe hard and trying to get control of the shakes that had set in. In a few minutes I was OK. I checked the apartment that the porch belonged to. The curtains were shut, but no lights were on inside. Now, if only the glass door isn't locked, I thought.

It wasn't. When you think of it, why would someone lock a door that is four floors up in the air? The rooms of the apartment were just the same as Larry's place. I let myself out the front door and into the hall. There was no way I would take a car down to the ground floor. I could run right into Rat Face. I took the stairs and went out the way I had come in.

I stood in the dark behind the building and worked to get some kind of plan set in my mind. I had $30, no car, and outside of Larry, didn't know anyone in the whole state of California. I had the papers Larry gave me; they were in my jeans pocket. But I didn't know what they were. I had not even looked at them.

"Wait a minute," I said aloud. "I *do* know somebody in California!" I walked about a half mile to where I found some eating places. There was a telephone booth outside a McDonald's. I got some change and took out the little piece of paper from my notebook. I punched out Sue Conway's number.

She answered on the second ring. "Sue?" I said. "This is Jim Singer. Remember me?"

"How could I forget you?" she said. "You saved my life. But I didn't think I would hear from you so soon. I just got home a few hours ago."

"I know this sounds strange, Sue," I said,

"but I'm in a bad spot here. I didn't have any one else I could call."

"I thought your uncle was meeting you. What happened?"

"It would take too long to tell you on the phone. Look, do you know someone with a car?"

"Sure—me. Dad's car. He can't drive it, but I can."

"Great!" I said. "Listen, Sue. I'm in Pasadena. Can you get here and pick me up?"

"I guess so. Dad is asleep. But you are far away. It will take me an hour to get there."

"I have nothing but time, Sue."

"If I come out there, you better have a good reason for all this," she said.

"I'll explain everything when you get here," I told her. But I didn't know where *here* was. I looked over at a street sign at the end of the block. "I'm at the McDonald's on Colorado."

"Colorado and where? What is the cross street?"

"I don't know. I can't see the sign from here. But there is a music store on the corner called The Guitar Center. The street number on the window is 845."

"Good enough," Sue said. "I can look it up on one of Dad's maps. See you in about an hour, Jim."

"I'll be here."

She hung up, and I went inside the McDonald's to wait. I was on my third cup of coffee when she walked in the door an hour later. She had changed clothes and cleaned up. She had looked good on the train, but now she was the best thing I had ever seen. I got her a cup of coffee and then began to explain. Twenty minutes later she looked at me and shook her head.

"You know, Jim," she said, "for someone who just got into town, you sure got into trouble fast. Have you looked over those papers your uncle gave you?"

"No. He said they were important. I guess it is some FBI thing."

"Did he tell you not to look at them?"

"No . . . "

"Then let's see them. Maybe there is something in them that will tell us what is going on. It seems that the man you called Rat Face really wants to get you—or the papers."

I opened the two pieces of paper onto the table. One was covered with numbers and

25

strange letters. The other was filled with names and addresses and some phone numbers. "Make any sense to you?" I asked Sue.

"Not a bit. It does not look like anything I ever learned in school."

"What about the names and numbers on the other paper?"

"Dead end, I'm afraid. Not one of them is in this part of California. I can tell by the phone numbers. And you have no idea where your uncle is?"

I reached over and took her hand. "Sue, I don't even know if he is alive. I didn't want to say it . . . or even think it. I don't know what to do. I don't know where I am. And the only person I know is you."

"Lucky me!" She laughed, and maybe it was nerves, but I did too. Maybe much longer and harder than I should have.

Then she quit laughing and said, "I have it. If Rat Face is after these papers, there is only one place for us to keep them safe."

"Don't keep me guessing," I said. "Where?"

"The Los Angeles FBI office. And they would also know what is going on with your uncle. He works for them."

"Why didn't I think of that?" I said. "Not that I would know where the office is or how to get there."

"Not to worry. I do. It is in the Federal Building in Westwood. Let's go." She got up from the table.

"It is after eleven at night. Will they be open now?"

"I don't know. I thought the FBI was like the police: open 24 hours. But we can find out when we get there."

"Just a minute," I said. "I have to make a phone call first."

"I thought you didn't know anyone here."

"I don't. I'm going to leave a message about what I'm doing. My uncle has an answering machine. In case he *is* all right, at least he will know what I did and that the papers are safe."

"Clever boy. I'll get my car."

She pulled up at the phone booth in a 1968 Pontiac GTO that looked like it had just rolled off the line. "Great car," I said as I got in. "Who did all the work on it?"

"What work?"

"The body and paint job. Sorry. It's my line of work, you know."

She laughed. "It came this way. Dad

bought the car new, and it was always his pet. He took good care of it."

"I'll say."

Sue drove the Pontiac onto Colorado Boulevard, and in a few minutes we were on a freeway going west. Half an hour later we pulled into a parking place outside the Federal Building. Most of the lights in the tall building were out. We parked and made for the front door. We were just going up the steps when I thought I heard something behind us. I turned and nearly went through the ground. It was Rat Face, and he had a gun!

"Freeze," Rat Face said. "Both of you. This is no toy gun."

4

Sue let out a little cry and took my arm. Rat Face waved the gun. "Inside," he said. I could not believe it.

"You do know the FBI office is in this building, don't you?" I asked.

"I should," he said, reaching into his coat pocket. He took out an ID card with his picture on it. "I'm an FBI agent. Come on you two, inside."

We went. He had a key to one of the cars that lined the inside hall. We got in and he waved us off when we got to the sixth floor. The office we entered was almost shut down. There were a lot of desks but no one at them. There were only a few lights on. At the end of the room was a big wood door. Rat Face moved us toward it. When we got there, I read the name plate on the door: Eugene Croft—Regional Director. Rat Face knocked, opened the door, and pushed us through the doorway.

Seated at a big white desk was a man of about 50. He had no more hair than an egg, and he looked up at the three of us with bright gray eyes that seemed to go right through me.

"Got them, Mr. Croft," Rat Face said.

"So I see, Turner," Croft said. "Who is the girl?"

"I don't know yet. She drove young Singer right here."

"What about the papers?" Croft asked.

"I have them," I answered. "What is all this about? Where is my uncle?"

"One thing at a time," Croft said. "Give me the papers first."

I gave them to him. He turned on a very bright light on his desk and took out a strong hand glass. Then he picked up a letter opener and began to pick at the papers. What was going on?

"Are they all there, boss?" asked Rat Face.

"Seem to be," Croft answered and kept picking at the papers. He looked up. "Yes, they are all here. Lucky for you, Turner. You have made a mess of this whole business, you know."

"I did get young Singer, boss."

"That was just dumb luck. If that message wasn't on the answering machine, would you have ever found him? All you had to do was wait for him to show up."

"Will you two stop talking about me like I wasn't here?" I said. "Look—I have been all over this town all day. I had to sell my father's watch just for some cash. I have not had a bath in two days, and my clothes must smell by now. I almost killed myself trying to get away from"—I broke off; I had almost called Turner Rat Face—"this man here," I went on. "I'm tired, dirty, and more than a little screwed up by all this. And I think it is only fair now for you to tell me what this is all about. I gave you the papers, didn't I?"

"The papers are nothing," Croft said. He

pointed the letter opener to a bunch of black spots on the white desk top. "See those? That is what we were after."

"That explains nothing to me."

"Those black spots were the dots on some of the letter *i*'s on the papers. They are really small pictures taken with a special camera. Put them in a special machine, and you see what is on those pictures."

"And what *is* on them?" I asked.

"You don't have to know," Croft said shortly.

"And where is my uncle?"

"I wish I knew. But we will pick him up sooner or later."

"But why? He works for you, right?"

Croft laughed: a hard sound, like a dog barking. "You just don't get it, do you, Singer? Your uncle used to work for us. But he has gone bad. Those little pictures were going to be sold to another government. Now that we have them, we will go after your uncle. And you are going to help us do it."

"Wait a minute. All I have is your word for this. And what about my friend here? She does not know anything about this. Not that I do, either." Sue moved toward me, and I put my arm around her.

"If she is clean, she can go home," Croft said. "Give us some ID, young woman, and we can have you checked out in an hour's time. Our machines are very fast, and they run all night." He put out his hand. Sue reached into her handbag and took out her driver's license.

"This is all I have," she said.

"It will be enough," Croft told her. He handed the license to Turner. "Run this through the machine right away," he told Rat Face. "And while you are on the fourth floor, pick up a watch for young Singer here. I think he is going to need it."

"Thanks, but I can get my father's watch back," I said. "I know where to find the man I sold it to. He is a drug dealer at Union Station."

Croft smiled. "You make friends fast, Singer. In town one day and already you know the best people. Tell me more about this man." He took out a pen and a piece of paper.

I told him the whole story: everything that had happened since I got off the train. I even told him how I had met Sue Conway and how she had helped me. By the time I was done, Turner had come back.

"The Conway woman is clean so far as we can tell, boss," Turner said to Croft.

"I was pretty sure she was, from what Singer has told me. By the way, he had no idea who you were. Why didn't you show him your ID card?"

"I never could get near enough. He runs fast. And I don't know how he gave me the slip at the apartment house."

"I do," Croft said. "I'll tell you later." He gave me a small, dry smile. "Did you bring the watch, Turner?"

"Right here."

"Give it to Singer."

It was a new black sports watch, the kind with a timer and a counter. "But I'll get my own watch back," I began.

"You will wear this one. It is special. Sure, it keeps good time. But it also sends a radio sound we can follow. You turn it on by pushing the timer control. If you get into real trouble, push the other control. It will let us know that we need to come and get you out."

"Get me out of where? What is all this?"

"I told you. You are going to help us catch your uncle. If he thinks you still have the papers, he will get in touch with you. I am going to have new papers made just like these. But the dots on the i's will be phony.

"You go back to his apartment. He will most likely call you soon. He will want to meet you someplace. Say you will do it. Then call us at this number," he gave me a card from his desk top. "When you leave to meet him, push the timer control on your watch."

"Look, Mr. Croft," I said. "I'm no spy or anything like it. And my uncle is a good man. He helped my mother when my dad died. He even got me through school. Now you want me to set him up? After all the good he did for me?"

Croft smiled. "Stalin's daughter thought the world of her old man, too," he said. "That didn't stop him from being a monster, did it? And if you are not with us, Singer, I have to feel that you are against us. Maybe you were in on the whole deal. They put people away for that kind of thing, you know."

"That is a lie, and you know it!" I yelled.

"Easy . . . easy," Croft said. "I just said that maybe some people would think you were in on it. It would take many weeks to explain. Weeks you would spend away, if you know what I mean." He looked me right in the eye. "Well?"

"OK, you got me," I said. "But I don't like doing it."

"What makes you think I like doing it to you?" Croft said.

"How do I meet my uncle anyplace if I don't have wheels?" I asked. "And how do I get to his place?"

"I'm sure Miss Conway will drive you," Croft said.

"You leave her out of this," I yelled. "I'll do your dirty work for you. But let her go home now."

"It is all right, Jim," Sue said. "I'll drive you back. But it has to be soon. If Dad wakes up and needs some help, I should be there. It is very late."

And that is the way it all went down. Turner showed up with some papers just before we left. I could not tell them from the ones Larry had given me. Sue drove me to Larry's place, and we hardly talked at all. So much had happened so fast, there seemed little to say. As I was about to get out of the car, she put a hand on my arm.

"You are plenty of trouble, Jim," she said.

"But you are a good person." With this, she moved over toward me. "And if you call me again, let's just do that movie and have a bite to eat. No spy business, OK?"

"That is a deal. And I *will* call you. You can bet on it."

I got out, and she drove off. I went up to Larry's apartment. It was after one in the morning. Tired as I was, I wanted a bath more than sleep. I took a long hot one and went to bed. Just before I went to sleep, I kept thinking that Larry wouldn't get in touch. Telling Croft I would turn my uncle in was one thing; doing it was another.

5

The phone woke me at seven the next morning. I didn't get to it in time. The machine answered, and I heard Larry's voice. "Jim, this is me. I can't talk for long. Go downstairs to the mailbox, right away." Then he hung up.

I got out of bed and looked at the clothes I had been wearing for days. My clean things were still in Larry's Porsche someplace. Then I had a great idea. Larry and I are about the same build. Maybe some of his clothes would be all right on me. I went to the closet, and you should have seen what he had in there. Ten minutes later I looked like a clothes ad in *Sports Illustrated*.

I took the car down to the first floor and opened the mailbox with Larry's key. It was too early for the mail person to have been there. Inside was something cut from a newspaper: movie ads. One of the movie houses was marked in red. So was the time the movie was to begin. Larry's message was clear: Be at that movie house at the show time he marked—twelve noon.

I went back to the apartment to make some coffee and do some thinking. All of a sudden I had to decide if I was going to do what Croft told me to or not. It wasn't easy. If Croft made good on his promise, I would be in jail for weeks until I could be cleared. There would go my new job. I was to start on Monday and it was now Saturday.

Larry had been at the apartment building. He had to be the one who put the movie ad in the box. Why didn't he just come up and talk to me? Wasn't Rat Face or some other FBI man watching the place? Or was Croft so sure I would do what I was told that they left the place alone?

I made up my mind. Until I talked to Larry, there was no way I could turn him in. I would meet him and not tell Croft. Maybe I could talk to Larry and get him to give himself up. But first I had to find out where this movie house was. I checked the address on the ad. The place was in Pasadena. But the address didn't mean much to me. I would have to wait until the place opened and phone them to find out how to get there.

The ad said that the first showing was at noon. But the doors had to open before then. The time went slowly. Finally I got through. I was lucky I didn't get one of those machines. I got a real person on the line. He asked where I was calling from. That at least I knew. Turned out the place wasn't too far away. I could walk it.

When I got there, a line was already in place. Gangs of boys and a few girls were waiting to see the Clint Eastwood movie. I waited in line, and after a few minutes I went inside and found a seat in back, in the dark. The movie had not started. They were showing ads for what was going to play there next week. Suddenly I felt a touch from behind me. I heard Larry's voice.

"No, don't look around, Jim. Watch the movie," he said in a very low voice.

"I still have the papers, Larry," I said. I took them out of my pocket and passed them back. He held my wrist so hard I almost yelled.

"Where is your father's watch?" he growled.

"I had to sell it to get some cash," I explained. "When you left me, I had no money. Let go, will you? That hurts."

"I ought to tear your arm off," he said. "Why did you set me up?"

"Who says I did?"

"Come on, Jim. I knew what that sports watch was as soon as I saw it."

"It is true that they gave me the watch," I said. "And the papers are phony. They got the pictures. But I did my best to get away from them, Larry. I really did."

"Fool!" he said. "I *wanted* them to get those papers. I never thought you could give Turner the slip. You could turn out to be a good spy, Jim. Turner is a hard man to shake."

"But they have the papers. And the pictures."

"They only think they do. Those pictures

are as phony as the new papers they gave you. The real pictures are inside your father's watch." I felt his strong hand around the back of my neck. "Be sure you tell the truth now, Jim," he said. "You know I could break your neck with one move of my hand, don't you?"

"If you say so, I believe you."

"Just tell me where you sold the watch and who has it now."

In a few minutes I told Larry what had happened since he left me on the street in L.A. "And I didn't set you up," I said. "I didn't call Croft. He does not know I'm here."

He let go of my neck, and I started to breathe again. "Good, Jim. I'm going to let you live. I'm going now. You won't know when. You keep watching the movie. If you make a move toward that sports watch control, I'll have to change my mind."

"One thing," I said.

"What is it?"

"Why did you sell out?"

He laughed softly. "Did you see my apartment and my car? My clothes? You must like them; you are wearing some of them."

"Yes, I saw them all."

"Isn't it clear? I did it for the money."

I didn't say anything after that. Larry didn't say any more. I didn't even know if he was still behind me. I watched the movie. Clint Eastwood was going after a man who was trying to hide in an old building. Clint took out his gun. The other man had a gun, too. Shots rang out. But they sounded far away. The action in the movie didn't match the shots. They had come from outside the movie house!

I got up from my seat and walked up the aisle—right into Turner! "How did you get here?" I asked. "What were those shots? Is Larry . . . ?"

"He is all right. He took two bullets, but we got him."

"But I didn't use the watch. How did you find me?"

"We never thought you would. When you called this place to find out where it was, we knew where you were going."

"You were listening in on the phone line?"

"Every word. That's why Singer used the mailbox. Even we can't open that without papers from a judge."

"Why didn't you get him at the mailbox?"

"We had to stop watching the place. He has been in the business too long not to spot someone watching." Turner took my arm. "Let's get out of here. People are trying to watch the movie. We have someplace we have to go."

"Are you going to put me away for not telling you where Larry was meeting me?"

"Don't be silly. You did what we wanted, even if you didn't know. Nobody's going to give you a medal, but you are not in any trouble with us. No, we're going to spend some time with my boss. The pictures were phony. We have find out where the real ones are."

I laughed. "Now that is something I *do* know," I said.

Eight hours later, I was at Union Station, walking up to the coffee shop tables. Sure enough, Bunny was there doing business. He looked up as I came near.

"Hello, Bunny," I said. "Remember me?"

"Sure, man. I got your watch." He held up his wrist. He was still wearing it.

"I have the money," I said. "I want to buy it back."

"Well, I got a little surprise for you," he said. "The price just went up to $300. Besides, I see you already have another watch. One of those sports jobs."

"That is all right, Bunny," I said as I worked the control that would tell Turner and his men to move in. "I have a little surprise for you, too."

6

About three weeks later they let me go to the hospital to see Larry. Outside of the guard in the hall and the bars on the windows, it was like any hospital room. When I came in, Larry was in bed, and reading a book.

"Jimmy!" he said with a big smile. "How are you?"

"OK, I guess."

"How is the new job?"

"Just fine. They like my work."

"Are you still in my apartment? I'm paid up until the first of the year. No reason why you can't stay there."

"I'm going to move as soon as I can."

"Why?"

"I don't want to live on the money you sold out to get."

"Wait a minute. The money for my place was clean. So was the money for my car. But after I paid all that out, I didn't have anything left. I didn't go on the take until a few months ago. I was going to Brazil on *that* money.

"You can use that apartment and save the money you make at your job. You can have the Porsche, too. Where I'm going, I won't be needing it for some time." He laughed.

"You seem pretty happy for a man in your spot," I said.

"You know? In a way I'm glad it is over. Not that I look forward to jail. But I don't know if I could have spent the rest of my life on the run."

"Then why did you do it all? You were in Vietnam with Dad. You didn't sell out the country then. Why now?"

"All the time I was in Vietnam, all I wanted was to get home. When I did get back, what did I come home to? The whole world just wanted to forget my dirty little war. It was like I threw away those years of my life for nothing."

"Dad didn't sell out."

"He didn't have a thing worth selling. He went back home and died because of that war. What did he end up with? A free piece of ground in Arlington? I knew things that were worth money. I saw my chance and took it.

"My country never cared about me; they showed it. No one cared for the men who went to fight. And when we came home, no one wanted to know us. Don't wave a flag at me, Jim. I'm past all that." He turned his face to the wall near his bed.

"I'm sorry, Larry," I said.

"So am I," he said. "I'm more sorry than you will ever know. I got caught." He was still looking at the wall when I left the room.

I was feeling low as I left the hospital. I got a bus headed for Pasadena. By now I could get around well on the buses. But I got to thinking I had to phone Croft and Turner to find out where Larry's car and keys were.